The Day the Circus Came to Lone Tree

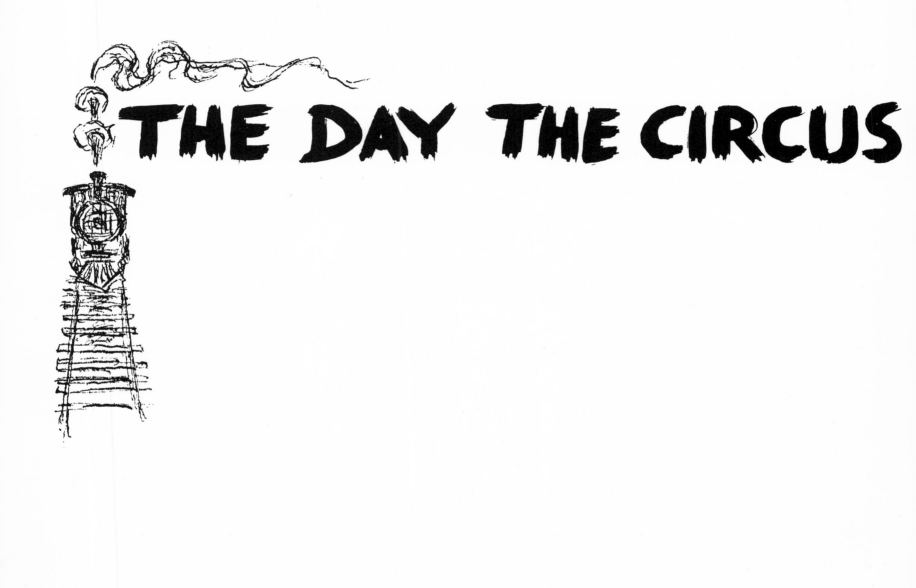

THE DAY THE CIRCUS

CAME TO LONE TREE

BY GLEN ROUNDS

HOLIDAY HOUSE • NEW YORK

Copyright © 1973 by Glen Rounds
Printed in the United States of America
All rights reserved

Library of Congress Cataloging in Publication Data

Rounds, Glen, 1906–
  The day the circus came to Lone Tree.

  SUMMARY: The circus has never gone back to
Lone Tree after the events of their first visit.
  [1. Circus stories] I. Title.
PZ7.R761Daz   [Fic]   73–78458
ISBN 0–8234–0232–0

Hardly a day goes by that someone doesn't stop me on the street to ask why the circus never comes here to Lone Tree.

The truth is that the circus *did* come to Lone Tree once many years ago. But almost nobody remembers it now, so of course they don't know what happened that day.

It was a simple misunderstanding that upset The Lady Lion Tamer's Act and caused all the trouble. The people who did what they did meant no harm; they were simply trying to be helpful. But the circus folk got pretty upset before the mix-up was straightened out, and to this day they absolutely refuse to even consider showing here again.

FOR THE TRUE STORY OF WHAT HAPPENED THAT DAY SO LONG AGO, READ ON.

At the time I speak of, Lone Tree was a busy, bustling cow town. Two trains a day (one in each direction) stopped there regularly. On Saturdays ranchers, cowboys, Indians, sheepherders, and homesteaders came from miles around to do their buying at Bearpaw Smith's Agency Store. It was his boast—and it might well be true—that he could furnish a body anything he might ask for, from a can of sardines to a top buggy with red wheels.

But there was one thing missing. Up to that time none of these good people—not even Sheriff Dan Dangerfield, who had been as far East as Chicago—had ever seen a circus.

Then one Saturday, just at noon, a stranger wearing city clothes drove into town and tied his horse to the hitchrack behind Bearpaw's Store. While a crowd gathered he unloaded rolls of paper, a paste bucket, and a long handled brush from the back of his buggy and laid them neatly on the ground before he set to work.

When he had arranged things to suit him, he dipped the brush into the paste bucket. Then standing on tiptoe in his pointed city shoes, he started spreading paste on the blank wall of the store, starting high up under the eaves and working downwards.

After that he unrolled one of the poster sheets, hung it on the end of his brush, and slapped it onto the pasted wall. With a few quick swipes he spread it flat, and as if by magic it suddenly turned out to be a brightly printed life-size picture of a lion.

Then in the same way, while the people milled about stepping on his carefully spread out sheets, kicking dust in his paste bucket, and asking questions by the dozens, the stranger spread sheet after sheet of the most amazing pictures the people of Lone Tree County had ever seen down the length of Bearpaw's Store.

There were pictures of ladies in skimpy dresses and pink tights, some riding fat white horses and others on elephants. There were pictures of clowns, trained dogs, seals, and sword swallowers. There were pictures of camels, zebras, lions, tigers, orangutans, and other creatures nobody knew the names of. Still not having said a word to anybody, the stranger finished his work, loaded his tools, and drove out of town. The people of Lone Tree were so busy discussing the posters that nobody noticed his going.

In the days that followed, the circus was talked about in bunkhouses, ranch houses, sod shacks, sheep wagons, Indian teepees, or any other place two or more people happened to meet.

Every day a crowd could be found beside Bearpaw's Store looking at the posters while folk who knew—or claimed to know—something about circuses instructed their less well-informed neighbors. Even at night late comers stood about looking at the pictures by the smoky light of high held kerosene lanterns. The excitement was almost more than the people could bear.

But the day did come at last. When that circus train pulled onto the Lone Tree siding, just at sunrise, there were nearly two hundred buggies and wagons lined up hub to hub on the flats along the track. And the cattle pens and loading chutes threatened to collapse from the weight of men and boys perched on the top rails. Horses, frightened by the locomotive and the strange smells from the circus cars, reared and plunged. Riders were thrown, buggies and wagons tipped over, and women and children thrown underfoot. But in spite of all the excitement, no real damage was done.

While the confusion straightened itself out, the work of unloading and setting up the circus got under way. Everywhere people gathered in clusters to marvel at the strange sights. Men and boys on horseback constantly rode back and forth between the show grounds and the siding, trying to see everything at once.

Families peered into the shadowy interiors of cage wagons, marvelled at the strange sounds and smells, and spelled out the signs identifying the creatures inside.

Hunters, Indians, cowboys, and stockmen stared unbelievingly at giraffes and other equally improbable looking animals eating baled hay on the newly set up picket lines.

Already it was a day that nobody in Lone Tree County was soon to forget!

An hour before showtime the crowd on the midway and around the ticket wagon was already so great that it seemed impossible that the circus tent would be able to hold them all. And still the people came.

One of the late comers was Clyde Jones, the mountain lion hunter, with his pack of "lion hounds." The circus people said it was against the rules to take dogs into the tent. Clyde said his were the best hounds in the state, and where he went they went. The ticket taker answered that this was one place they were not going to go. If Clyde wanted to see the circus, he'd have to leave his dogs outside. Clyde grumbled, but he did want to see the circus, so he tied the hounds to tent stakes and left them howling after him as he went inside.

Just then the Ringmaster in black boots, a high silk hat and long red coat gave the signal for the circus to start. The band played loud music. Clowns ran about distracting people's attention from the parade of horses, camels, elephants, and ladies and foreign looking performers—all dressed in feathers, sequins, and other glittering trappings of a magnificence no one there had ever seen before.

The people of Lone Tree County sat spellbound while high overhead, next to the very top of the tent, performers flew incredible distances through the air from one flimsy trapeze to another.

They cheered and applauded the elephant acts, the clowns, and the dog and pony shows. They drank soda pop and ate peanuts, popcorn, and cotton candy. Nowhere had the circus people ever had such an appreciative audience, and already the manager was thinking about showing in Lone Tree every year.

Then, a high steel cage was set up in the center ring, and the Ringmaster introduced "LINDA, the world's only LADY LION TAMER, and her collection of fierce and dangerous LIONS and TIGERS!"

The band played brave music while Linda the Lady Lion Tamer bowed and smiled at the crowd. The people sat up straight in their seats while circus men carrying long prod poles took places around the outside of the cage. When everything was ready, the lions and tigers were prodded through the chute from the menagerie tent and came roaring into the cage where the little lady stood with only a small chair in one hand and a whip in the other.

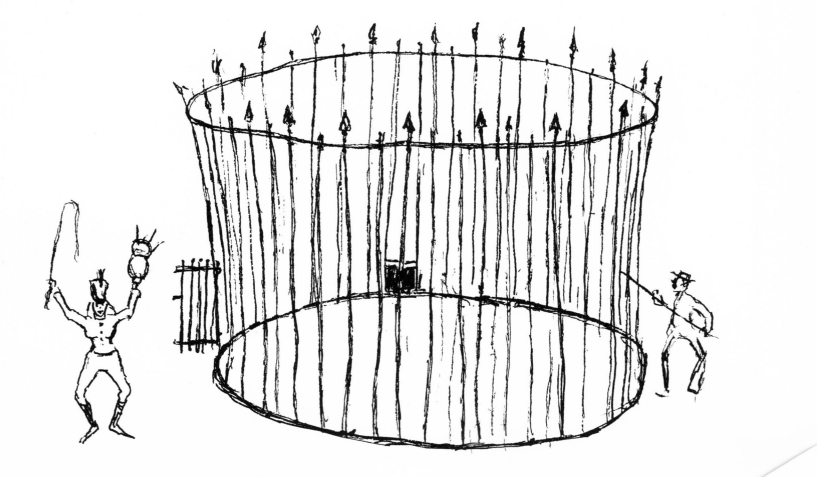

For a minute the Lady Lion Tamer appeared to be standing waist deep in a swirling confused mass of big cats. Then, with shrill commands and much cracking of her whip, she began to put them through their paces. First she ran them round and round the cage, from left to right. Then she turned them about and made them run from right to left. She made them jump up and sit on tubs, then made them get down and change places with one another. She made one lion lie down and play dead, wrestled with another, and made a tiger jump through a flaming hoop. Never had the people of Lone Tree, sitting breathless on the edges of their seats, seen or imagined the things they saw there.

Then, just as she was lining the big cats up on a row of high pedestals, one huge old lion refused to obey! When she repeated the command and cracked her whip, he only bared his yellow fangs, snarled, and batted at the lash with his paw. Ignoring both the repeated commands and the cracking of the whip, the great beast, belly to the ground and tail switching from side to side, began slowly creeping closer and closer to the Lady Lion Tamer.

By this time the people of Lone Tree, thinking she was in danger, were on their feet, but still the men with prod poles paid no attention to what was going on inside the cage.

Meanwhile the Lady Lion Tamer shifted both chair and whip to her left hand and drew a small nickel-plated pistol from her belt. Aiming dead between the great beast's eyes, she pulled the trigger. The lion only shook his head, snarled, and crept a little closer. Twice more she fired that little pistol while the circus men leaned against the bars and did nothing.

Finally the Lone Tree cowboys could stand it no longer! If the circus people wouldn't rescue the little lady from that dangerous beast, they would do it themselves. So, yelling shrill cowboy yells, they pulled their hats firmly down on their heads, drew their own pistols, and swarmed down into the arena.

The circus people were hollering and carrying on about something or other, but the cowboys were too busy trying to find a way into the cage to pay them any mind.

A quick-thinking rider ran for his horse tied outside, shook out his throw rope, threw a loop over a top bar of the cage and pulled an entire section away. Clyde's mountain lion hounds had chewed their ropes in two and joined the cowboys just as they crowded through the opening the rider had made.

Tigers snarled and yowled, lions roared, hounds bayed, and cowboys whooped and fired their pistols indiscriminately into the swirling clouds of dust. And all the while the band went on playing loud music.

For a time the excitement and confusion were considerable!

Meanwhile, back in the menagerie tent, the other animals were beginning to be upset by the uproar. The elephants, trumpeting and squeaking, pulled up their picket stakes. Then, as they blundered about trying to find a way out of the tent, they overturned cage wagons, and generally created a great disorder. In almost no time at all, animals of a dozen kinds had followed them through great holes ripped in the canvas walls and were stampeding out across the prairie in all directions.

As soon as the cowboys discovered that the circus animals were loose, they ran for their horses. Shaking out their ropes, they rode out to bring the escaped animals back.

Cowboys are very obliging that way—and besides, they might never again have a chance to try out their ropes and cowhorses against tigers, elephants, kangaroos and such. It was a chance no cowboy could resist.

The men of Lone Tree County were expert ropers—there were probably none better anywhere—and they planned to rope and hog tie the escaped circus animals just as they were in the habit of doing with the long-horned cattle on the range.

But to their surprise, this seemingly simple project turned out to be somewhat more difficult than they'd expected. For one thing the strange appearance, smells, and sounds of the unfamiliar livestock frightened their horses, making them almost unmanageable.

And there were other unexpected problems.

Birdlegs Smith, Sam Plentyshirts, and Olin Bagley—all expert team ropers —set out to catch a running elephant. Working together with the smoothness they'd learned in a hundred rodeos, Birdlegs dropped his loop neatly over the creature's head while Sam snared the near front foot and Olin did the same with the off rear. As soon as the three nooses had been twitched snug, the well-trained horses squatted on their haunches, bracing themselves for the coming shock.

The ropes, snubbed firmly to the saddle horns, snapped taut from the elephant's weight—but instead of being thrown, as would have been the case with a running longhorn, this creature didn't even hesitate. With ears spread wide and carrying both trunk and tail straight up he simply kept on running.

Birdlegs' cinch broke from the shock and still in the saddle he sailed high in the air at the end of the rope, which he unfortunately had tied to his saddle horn in the Texas fashion. Olin's horse was jerked from his feet. Meanwhile Sam's horse was spooked at the sound of the elephant's trumpeting and began to buck.

So they all ended up on the ground among the cactus, and the last they saw of the elephant he was leaving the country in a cloud of dust, dragging three ropes and a good Forth Worth saddle behind him.

But when they had pulled themselves together and looked around, they discovered they were not the only ones in trouble.

Off to one side Highpockets Hedges was trying to get his rope on a kangaroo. But every time he dropped a noose over the creature's head it simply leaped straight up in the air and escaped.

Nearer by Woodrow Bridges had caught a tiger, and as they watched, it was doing its best to climb into the saddle with him.

Trying to escape the angry tiger, Woodrow's horse blundered into the ropes of Cropear Simpson and Curly Wilson, who were doing their level best to throw and hog tie a camel.

The uproar that followed was something to see and hear. Men, horses, tigers, and camels, all indiscriminately entangled in a cat's cradle of ropes and blinded by the rising cloud of dust, trying to extricate themselves while crying out at the tops of their voices—each in his own fashion.

Everywhere they looked cowboys were struggling with strange animals and coming off second best, or limping through the sagebrush trying to catch rider-less horses.

All in all, it was a torn, bruised, scratched, and unhappy bunch of cowboys that finally gave up and started back for town. Some walked, some walked and carried scarred saddles, while others rode double behind friends who had not lost their horses.

They met the circus men, who had repaired broken cages and were on the way to catch the escaped animals in their own way. The circus folk didn't return the cowboys' greetings or answer when they offered to go along and help.

All night long the people of Lone Tree, from the hill north of town, could see the lights of bobbing lanterns and hear the strange cries as the circus people searched the plain for their animals. It was dawn before the last tiger was in his cage and the last elephant coaxed up the ramp into the animal car. Just as the sun came up the circus train pulled out, and was never seen there again.

The people of Lone Tree had enjoyed the circus so much and had tried so hard to be neighborly and helpful, they couldn't understand why none of the circus people would even wave good-bye.

The cowboys didn't mean to stampede all the circus stock; they just didn't realize that the lion was only doing what he had been trained to do and that the Lady Lion Tamer was really in no more danger than usual.

But even so, the fact is that from that day to this the circus absolutely refuses to even consider showing in Lone Tree. They don't even answer letters from there.

Glen Rounds knows the West intimately. He was born in the Badlands of South Dakota, spent his boyhood on a ranch in Montana, and after that "prowled the country" as a mule skinner, cowpuncher, logger, carnival talker, sign painter, and lightning artist.

His career as author-illustrator began more than thirty years ago with the publication of OL' PAUL, THE MIGHTY LOGGER. Since that time he has published a number of books, most of them about the West. He has an unerring eye for the significant characteristics of his subjects, which he depicts in phrase and brush stroke with sympathy, vitality, and humor.

Mr. Rounds now makes his home in Southern Pines, North Carolina.